Curious Sara

questions everything

Written by Kathi Bertoldie

Illustrated and Designed by Fx And Color Studio

About the Author

Kathi's goal is simple, to write children's picture books that kids enjoy, are fun to read aloud and don't take themselves too seriously.

Kathi loves being a Stay-at-Home mom of two children, a beautifully spirited daughter named Sara, to whom this book is named, and an amazingly wonderful and kind teenage son named Jack. She currently lives in Ozark, Missouri. As a devoted mom, she knows how special the time spent reading stories to a child can be. The way their faces light up when they hear the words and see the illustrations is magical! Kathi wanted to share with other kids the fun and excitement her children experienced listening to her story about Sara and Fred! She hopes your family enjoys her book as much as she has enjoyed writing it.

Ricky, Jack and Sara

My dream is finally coming true and it's all because
you believed in me.

I believe in you, too. Always remember that.

Why does the moon come out only at night?
Why do the stars shine so bright?
Why is the darkness full of such fright?
I think I know why, but really, not quite.

Why are red roses so fragrant and sweet?
Why do crisp leaves crumple under my feet?

Why are blue gumballs such a wonderful treat?
Well, I'm not so sure, but really, it's neat!

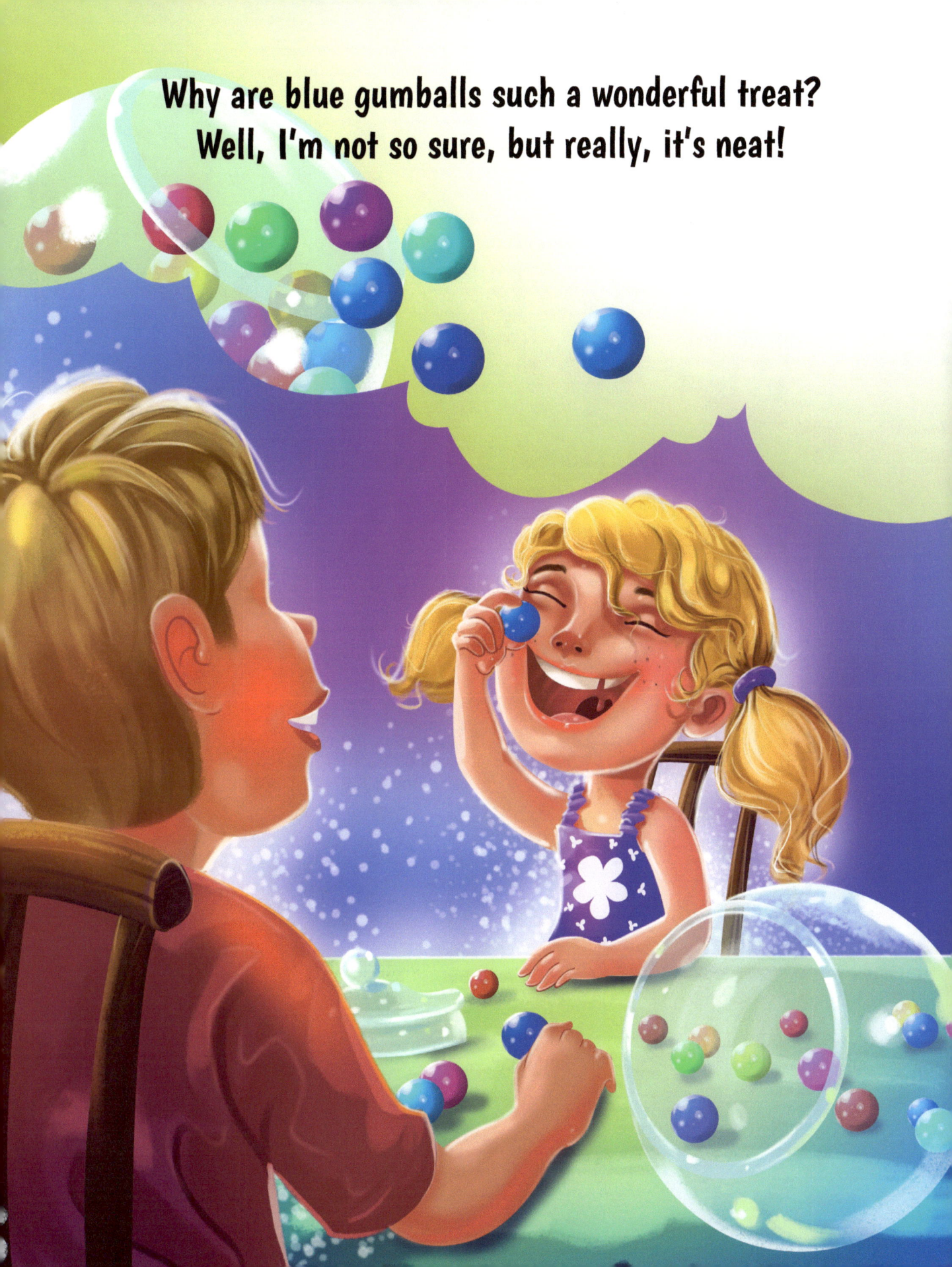

Why do moms love you
and care for you so?

Why do dads hug you when
you're feeling low?

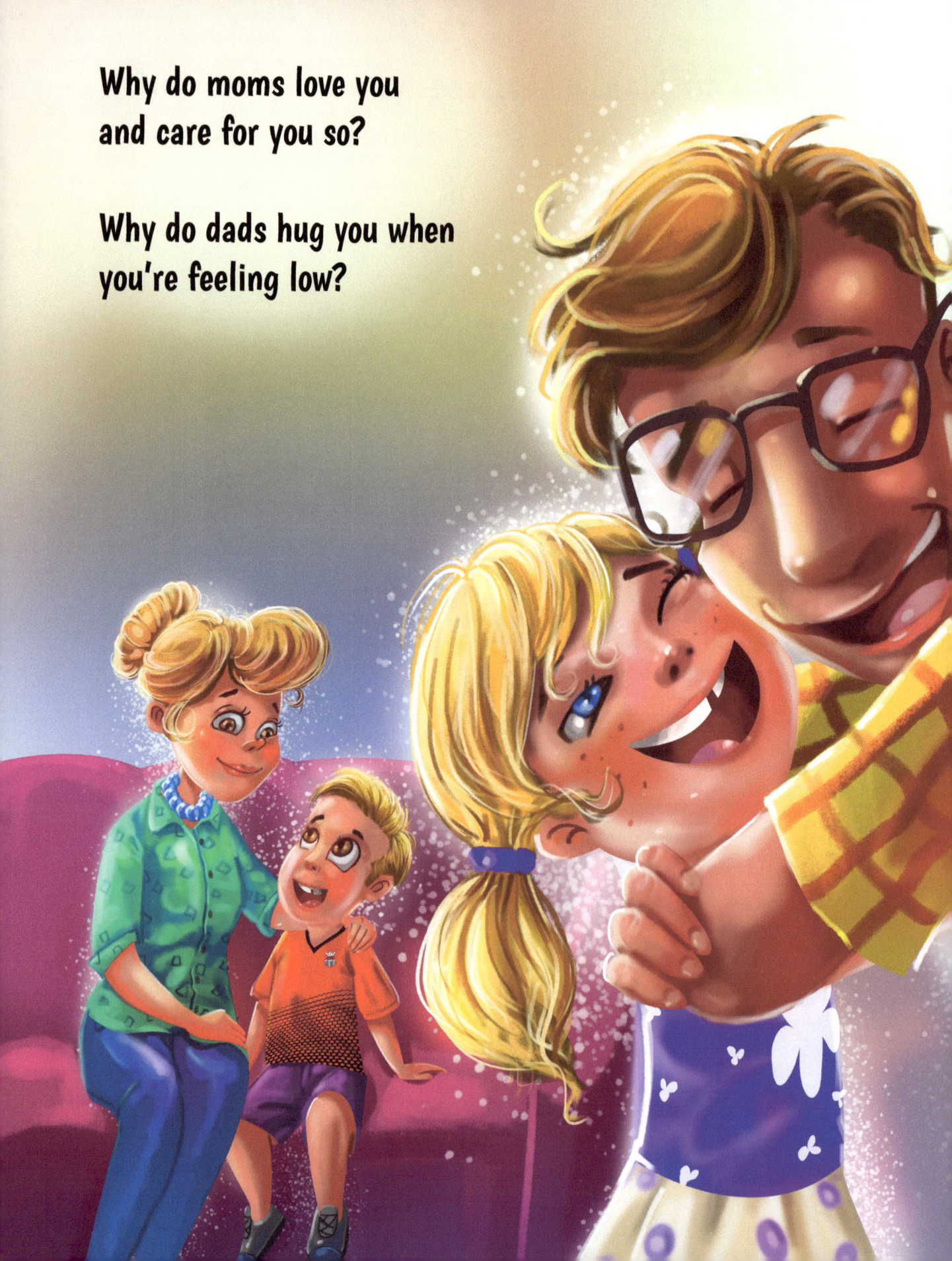

Why do yucky vegetables help me to grow?
I could make up a story, but then, I'll never know.

There were lots of good questions inside my big head.
I thought of them often while lying in bed.

I tossed and I turned! Then, I asked brother Fred.
He is much older and here's what he said...

Dear sister Sara, be sure not to wonder
Why there are things such as lightning and thunder.

All of your questions have one simple truth.
I know all the reasons and even have proof!
I saved up my money and hired a sleuth
And found all the answers when I was a youth!

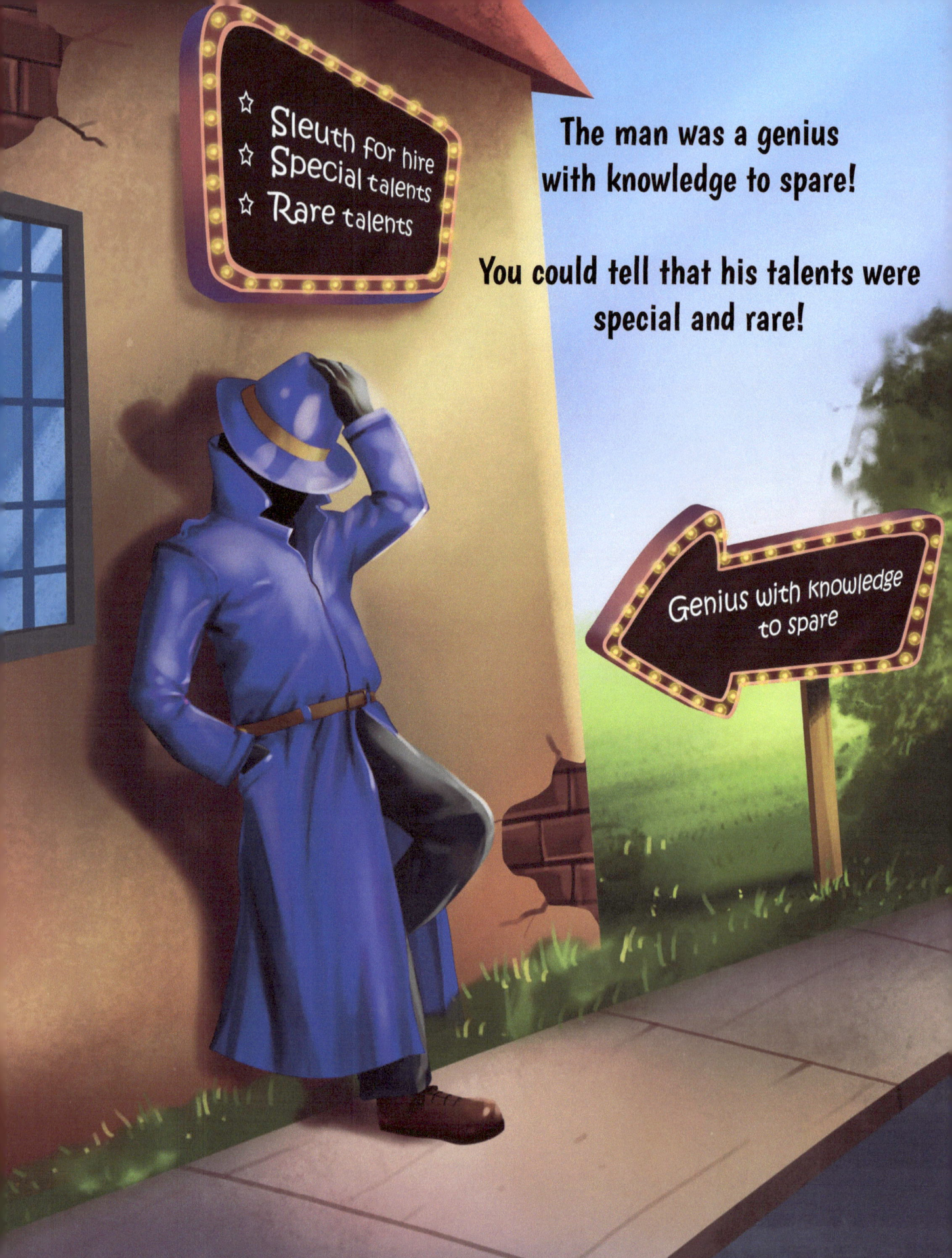

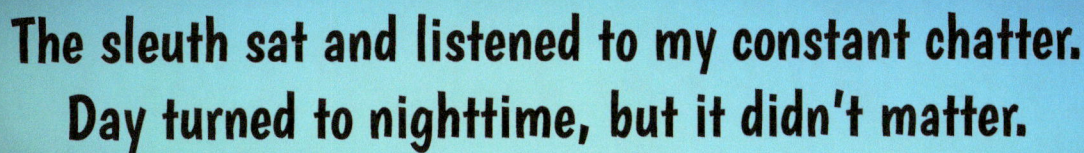

The sleuth sat and listened to my constant chatter.
Day turned to nighttime, but it didn't matter.

I could even start feeling my brain getting **FATTER!!**

Then, I waited with patience...
like a major league batter!

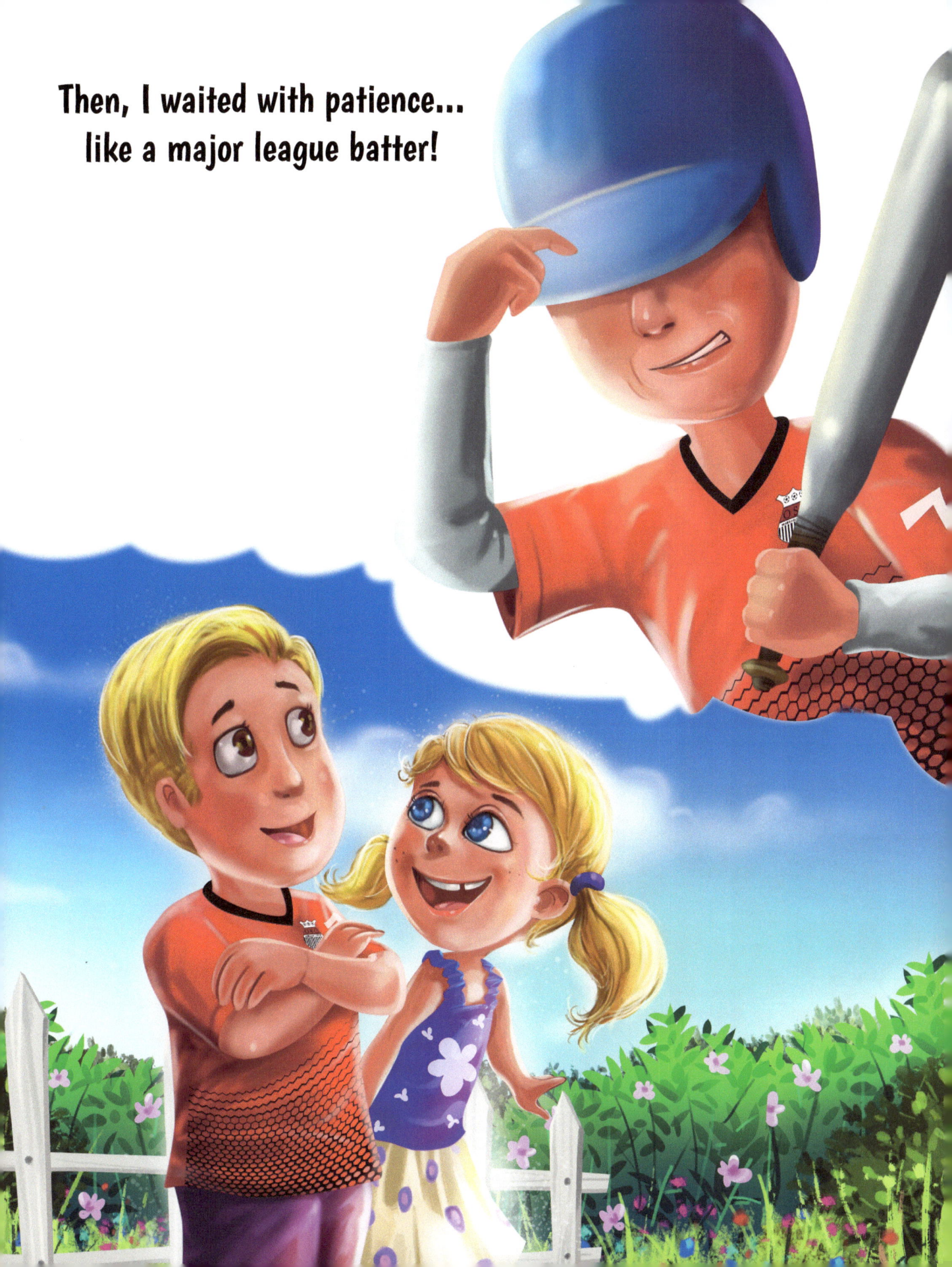

I waited...and waited...and waited...

...and waited...and waited...

Then....the man started speaking with care and great ease.
When he was through talking, I was really quite pleased.

I even could tell you why kittens get fleas!
Dear sister Sara, it's simple!

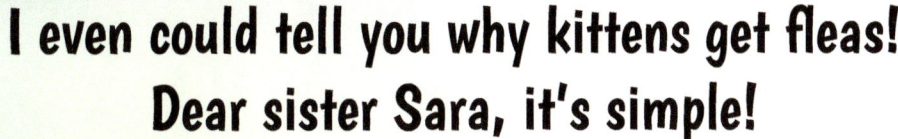

www.ingramcontent.com/pod-product-compliance
Lightning Source LLC
Chambersburg PA
CBHW041007170626
46815CB00002B/204